essential careers™

CAREERS IN MENTAL HEALTH

DANIEL E. HARMON

Rosen YA™
New York

Published in 2018 by The Rosen Publishing Group, Inc.
29 East 21st Street, New York, NY 10010

First Edition

Library of Congress Cataloging-in-Publication Data

Names: Harmon, Daniel E., author.
Title: Careers in mental health / Daniel E. Harmon.
Description: New York: Rosen Publishing, 2018. | Series: Essential careers | Audience: Grades 7–12. | Includes bibliographical references and index.
Identifiers: LCCN 2017016578 | ISBN 9781538381540 (library bound) ISBN 9781508178859 (paperback)
Subjects: LCSH: Mental health services—Vocational guidance—Juvenile literature. | Mental health services—Vocational guidance.
Classification: LCC RA790.75 .H37 2018 | DDC 616.89/023—dc23
LC record available at https://lccn.loc.gov/2017016578

Manufactured in China

contents

INTRO

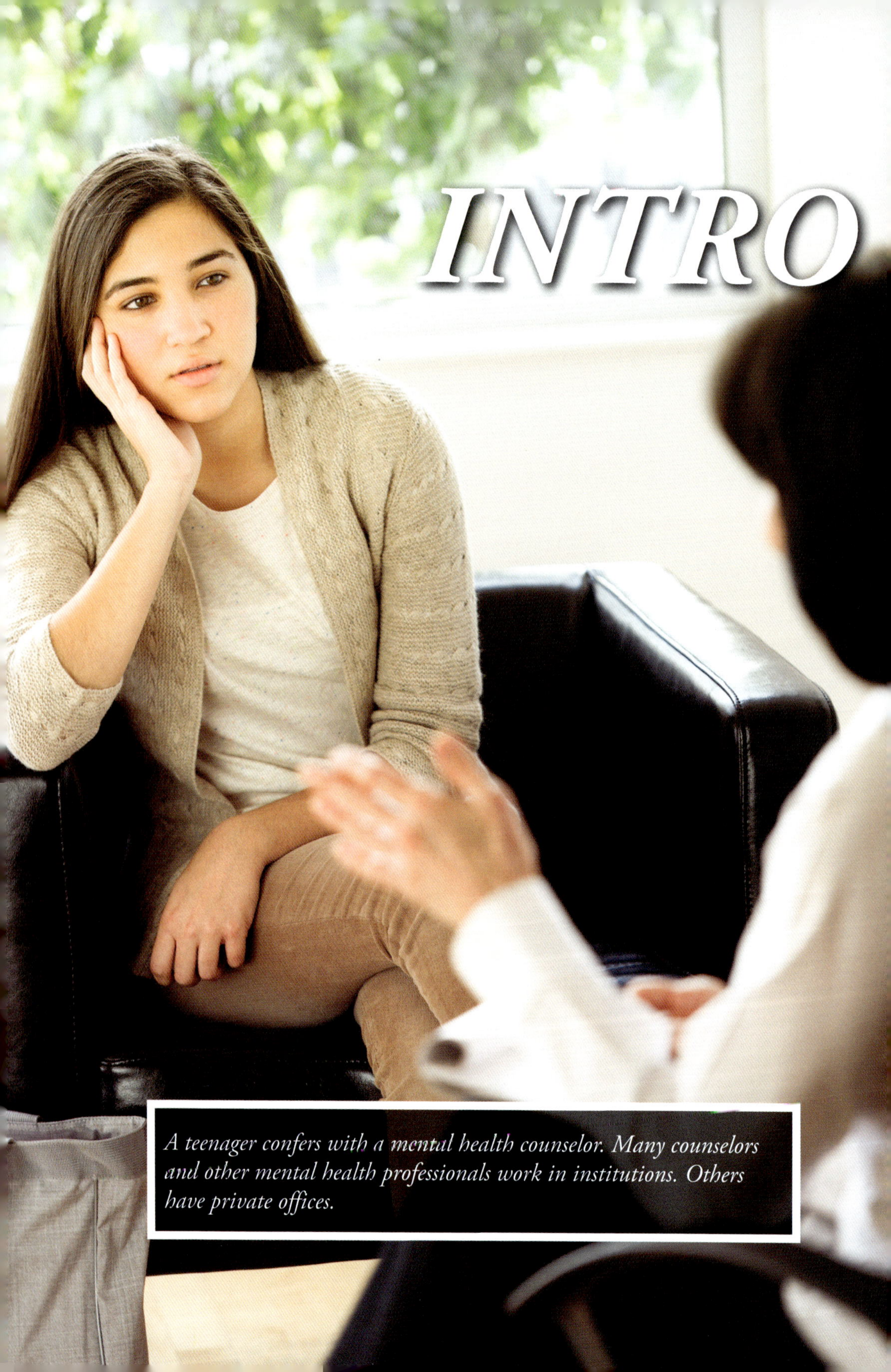

A teenager confers with a mental health counselor. Many counselors and other mental health professionals work in institutions. Others have private offices.

DUCTION

Sudden, violent outbursts. Schizophrenia. Hysteria. Hypochondria. Self-torture and starvation. Amnesia and other severe forms of memory loss. Hallucinations. "Crazy talk."

In centuries past, many individuals who suffered from any of those disorders were considered simply insane—by doctors as well as by people who knew them. If their behavior became extreme, injuring others or damaging property, they often were punished as common criminals. Many were imprisoned. Those whose everyday attitudes and actions were clearly unnatural were committed to asylums.

Asylums were facilities specially built to house people who were mentally disturbed. The public assumed inmates received more merciful treatment there than in prisons, including mental evaluations, medicine, and therapy. In reality, in most mental institutions the residents existed in misery. They received little effective treatment. The lives they led were as tortured, although in different ways, as those of dangerous criminals condemned to hard labor. Living conditions were squalid. Clinical, sanitized care was not the norm. Little progress was made in improving their mental and emotional conditions so they could return to society.

A mental disorder is a sickness with symptoms that cause serious distress in a person's thinking or behavior. It is brought about by brain malfunctions, caused either by biochemical or structural abnormalities. The main reason for the pitiful experience of asylum confinement prior to the twentieth century was that doctors and staff in those institutions understood little about mental illness. Only primitive medical studies had been performed in attempts to find effective medications and psychotherapy. Medicine generally consisted of a sedative to keep the person asleep or barely active.

Thankfully, giant strides have been made in mental health. Mental and medical health professionals now are able to treat a disorder with rehabilitation methods and medications precisely developed for that particular condition. They can improve the functioning and quality of life of most people who suffer from mental disorders. Patients can enjoy productive lives, residing and working in the community rather than being confined in hospitals. In many cases, patients can be cured.

Young people who are interested in a mental health career have many options to consider. Only a high school diploma is required for certain entry-level positions, such as psychiatric aides. Four-year college degrees are required for jobs as psychiatric technicians, behavioral disorder counselors, and social workers. Mental health counselors must have master's degrees. Psychiatrists are doctors with medical degrees. Psychologists are professionals with advanced degrees in psychology, either master's or doctoral degrees.

Workers in many other occupations regularly are involved in the care of mental health patients. Some work in hospitals. Others work in clinics, doctors' offices, residential patient institutions, and private homes. These workers include registered nurses and nurse practitioners, physician assistants, nursing assistants and orderlies, home health aides, and social and human service assistants. The nature of their work is not detailed in this resource; information can be found online in the *Occupational Outlook Handbook* that is produced by the US Bureau of Labor Statistics (BLS).

Mental health professionals are much in demand. The pay for most jobs in this field is above average. The personal satisfaction of helping people with mental disturbances, meanwhile, cannot be calculated.

chapter 1

Psychiatrists

Psychiatrists are the primary mental health physicians who diagnose and prescribe treatment for mental, behavioral, and emotional disorders. Their patients include people with psychotic disorders, anxiety, mood disorders, and addictions.

Psychiatrists begin a case by studying the patient's medical history and examining the individual in person. Usually, they order appropriate tests. They perform some tests themselves and have others administered by different mental health professionals.

After analyzing all the information, psychiatrists outline a plan of care that typically involves psychotherapy, hospitalization, and medication. Psychotherapy is a form of personal counseling in which the doctor schedules regular meetings with the patient to discuss problems and progress. Meetings sometimes are arranged with family members or with other patients who have similar issues.

The objective is to resolve or relieve the patient's problems. The psychiatrist may delve into past events or situations that might have triggered the disorder and may suggest behavioral changes. In typical cases, medication markedly improves and accelerates results. Medication may be available that can correct or reduce imbalances in the person's chemical makeup; such imbalances are common causes of mental disorders.

Many psychiatrists work in private practices, either alone or as members of a group of physicians. Some are affiliated

A doctor in the geriatric services section of a hospital works with a patient on brain exercises. Doctors and their staff members administer a variety of tests to analyze each patient's condition.

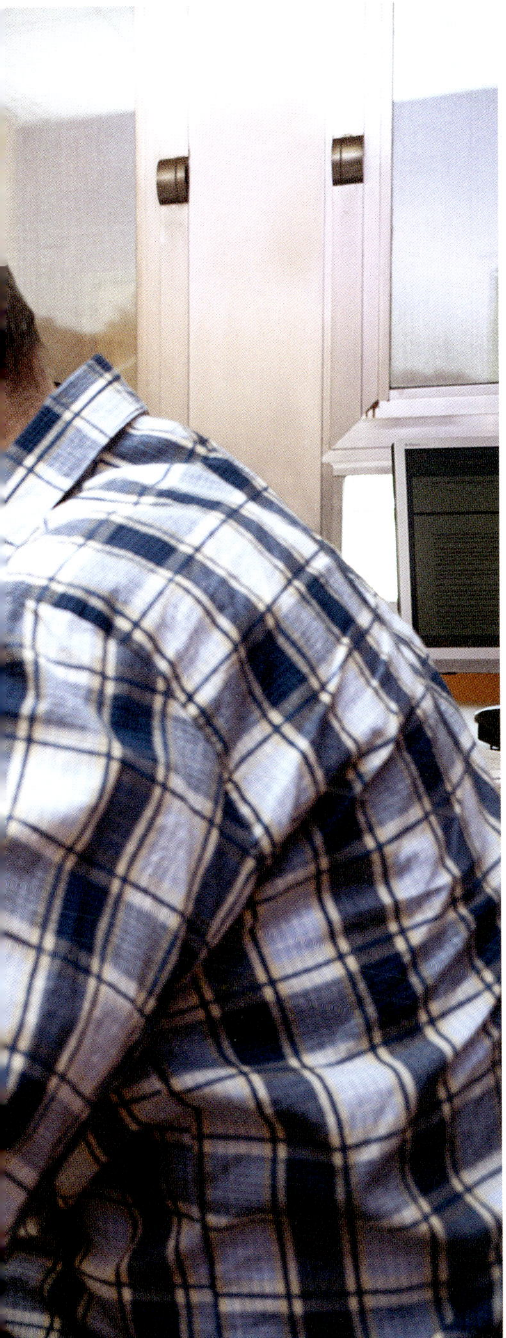

with mental health clinics, outpatient care centers, hospitals, or university medical centers. Psychiatrists usually are assisted by a team of health care professionals. Colleagues may include physician assistants, registered nurses, medical technicians, and medical record keepers. They monitor the effectiveness of medications and observe changes in the patient's behavior during the course of treatment.

Careers in psychiatry are promising. The need for new doctors in this field is expected to increase much faster than overall job growth, according to the BLS.

EDUCATION, TRAINING, AND CREDENTIALS

The path to becoming a psychiatrist is long and difficult. Students planning to become psychiatrists enter secondary studies as premedical students. They typically obtain a four-year degree in biology or another physical science. They take courses in humanities and

A medical team in a hospital meets to share notes and discuss suggestions. Different mental health specialists comprise the team assisting a psychiatrist.

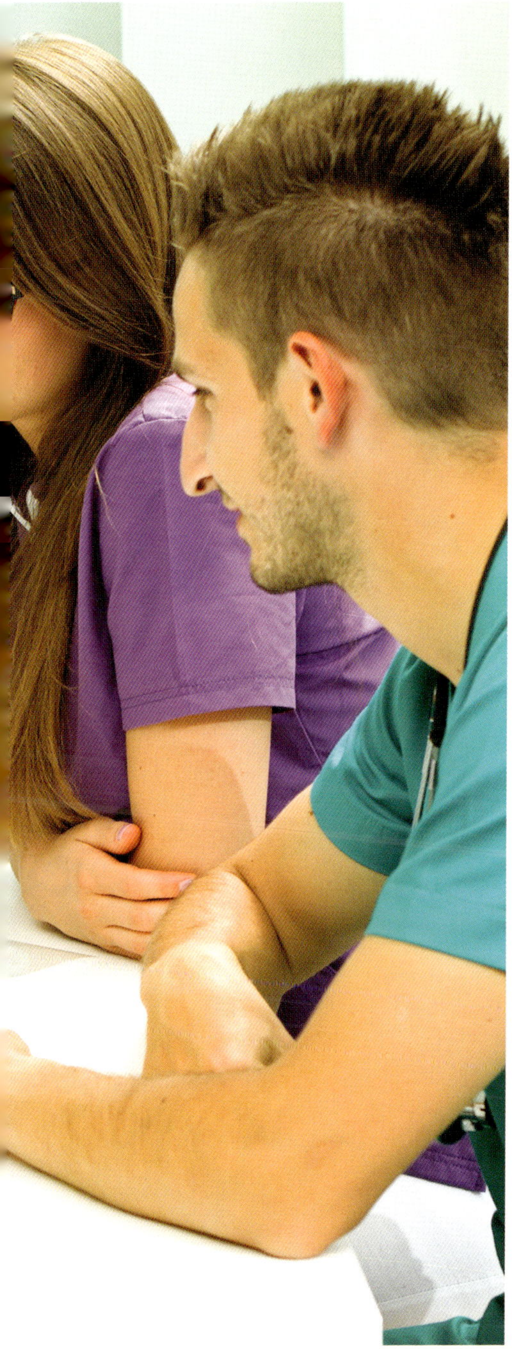

social sciences to learn about human conditions and interactions. To gain early training, they find internships or volunteer positions at medical institutions or clinics.

Graduation from a four-year program, even with good grades, does not ensure admission to an accredited medical school. Competition for entry is vigorous. An applicant must pass the standard Medical College Admissions Test. Admissions boards also consider leadership skills and other important personality characteristics. They require letters of recommendation from doctors or other medical professionals.

The first two years of a four-year medical school curriculum are heavy in studies of anatomy, pathology, and other biological sciences. During the last two years, students are involved in clinical rotations at hospitals and other medical facilities that are connected to the university. During this time, they observe doctors at work in different branches of medicine—surgery, pediatrics, oncology, and so forth—as well as psychiatry.

A World of Difference in Treatment

Psychiatrists and other mental health professionals receive better training today than ever before. The facilities where they work are better equipped and better staffed. Improvements over the years have made a world of difference for patients with mental disorders.

Well into the twentieth century, many psychiatric patients were placed in institutions in the company of other troubled inmates. Drinking water was polluted. Meals were hardly nutritious, by today's standards. Prolonged confinement in shackles and strait-jackets was common.

Sadly, in some countries, the mentally ill still are treated inhumanely. In developed societies, however, vast improvements have been made in treatment and care. Individuals who exhibit symptoms of a mental disorder are evaluated closely to determine the exact nature of their illness. Teams of trained personnel develop plans of treatment and care. Besides regular consultations with psychiatrists, psychologists, and other clinically licensed professionals, treatment typically includes one or more medications and different forms of therapy. Many patients can return to society and make valuable contributions.

Mental health administrators agree improvements are needed in this field of health care, but they cite encouraging progress over the years. Michael Friedman, adjunct professor at the Columbia University School of Social Work, recounted in a *Huffington Post* article his work in psychiatric rehabilitation in New York City during the 1970s. Most services for patients with severe, long-term disorders were "incredibly inadequate," and state hospitals by and large were "dreadful" and "often unsafe." Friedman concluded, "But what we have achieved … should be a source of pride in the vast improvements that have taken place over the past 40 years. And it should be a source of hope for the improvements that can be made over the next 40 years."

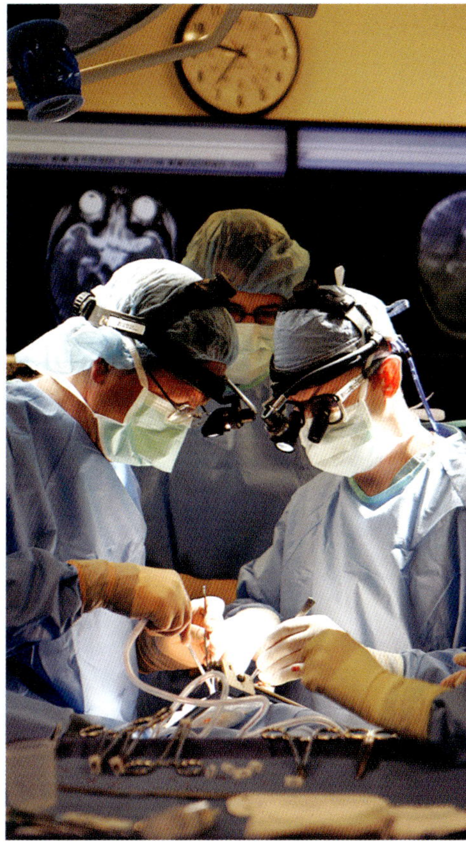

Medical students visit hospitals where they observe firsthand doctors at work in varying types of practice, including surgery, in addition to mental health treatment.

After successfully completing medical school, students are awarded doctor of medicine (MD) or doctor of osteopathic medicine (DO) degrees. To become a psychiatrist, they then begin a residency program in psychiatry at a hospital or mental institution. Residencies for psychiatrists take at least four years. Essentially, it consists of paid, on-the-job practice and learning under the mentoring of licensed psychiatrists. Residents study real-life cases involving different categories of psychiatric patients. They learn the various parts of the job, including consulting, testing, and treatment. They also work on academic projects and receive individualized training in psychotherapy and other clinical applications.

Like other physicians, psychiatrists must be licensed to enter professional practice. They take a standardized national licensure examination. Licensing requirements vary by state. They also may apply for certification by the American Board of Psychiatry and Neurology.

Some psychiatrists decide not to work directly with patients. They pursue careers in research, where they work in laboratories and perform clinical testing. Others prefer to teach, joining university faculties.

HANDS-ON TRAINING FOR MEDICAL STUDENTS

Students during the final two years of medical school are allowed to begin putting into practice the knowledge they've gotten from classroom studies. They are assigned what are known as clinical rotations. They follow doctors at teaching hospitals in the area. Along with their doctor-instructors, they interview and examine patients and participate in solving their medical problems.

Some medical schools provide preclinical courses that involve interacting with patients. This coursework equips students with important introductory experience for beginning their rotations.

Clinical rotations have an additional purpose besides providing personal contact with patients and opportunities to collaborate with doctors. The next step for students completing med school is a period of residency. Doctors and hospital administrators get to know students in their rotations. Frequently, they help graduating students secure residencies either at that hospital or at another one in the region.

During the period of clinical rotations, students accompany doctors in different disciplines. Teaming up like this gives them a firsthand idea of which discipline will best suit them. Typically, a medical school requires third- and fourth-year students to complete twelve four-week rotations each year. Psychiatry usually is among the core (fundamental) rotations. Students also participate in elective rotations in any medical specialty area.

Students in clinical rotations literally are in the process of becoming practicing physicians. When they graduate from medical school, they are ready to begin serving patients in the role of resident doctor.

PERSONAL QUALITIES

Psychiatrists, like all doctors, should be compassionate and patient. They must be able to supervise other medical workers and to communicate effectively with patients. They should be good listeners. An excellent command of English grammar and spelling is important; fluency in a second language may be necessary. They must be good organizers, critical thinkers, problem solvers, and decision makers and must be attentive to detail. They should be of an inquisitive, investigative disposition. They should be considerate and enjoy interacting with others. Psychiatrists must be prepared to handle stressful interactions. All doctors are independent minded but also compatible team workers.

Academically, physicians must be proficient in science and math. Mastering these basic classes in high school and junior high is very important for students who aspire to a medical career.

Technology skills will be needed for different aspects of the work. All physicians must be familiar with software systems to access medical records, medical research studies, and diagnostic information. They handle email on a daily basis. Some regularly use accounting and spreadsheet software.

chapter 2

PSYCHOLOGISTS

Psychologists study and document patients' mental and emotional processes and social behavior. Some of their patients have only short-term problems; others have chronic illnesses. Psychologists strive to understand patients' thought patterns, emotions, and actions. To do this, they gather information through methods including personal observation, interviews, surveys, and testing. Various tests are devised to provide insight into an individual's personality, intelligence, aptitude, and performance capabilities. Unlike psychiatrists, psychologists in most states are not allowed to prescribe medication for patients.

Different categories of psychologists are involved in the mental health field: clinical, counseling, developmental, social, and even forensic psychologists, who perform evaluations that are ordered through the criminal justice systems. Some work independently, others as part of health care teams. Almost a third are self-employed, according to the BLS. Those who work in hospitals and mental health centers serve in shifts, sometimes in the evening and on weekends. Those who practice independently set their own schedules, although they often work after normal working hours.

Clinical psychologists diagnose and treat mental disturbances as well as behavioral and emotional disorders. In addition to patient interviews, observation, and testing, they may work with patients in group or family psychotherapy

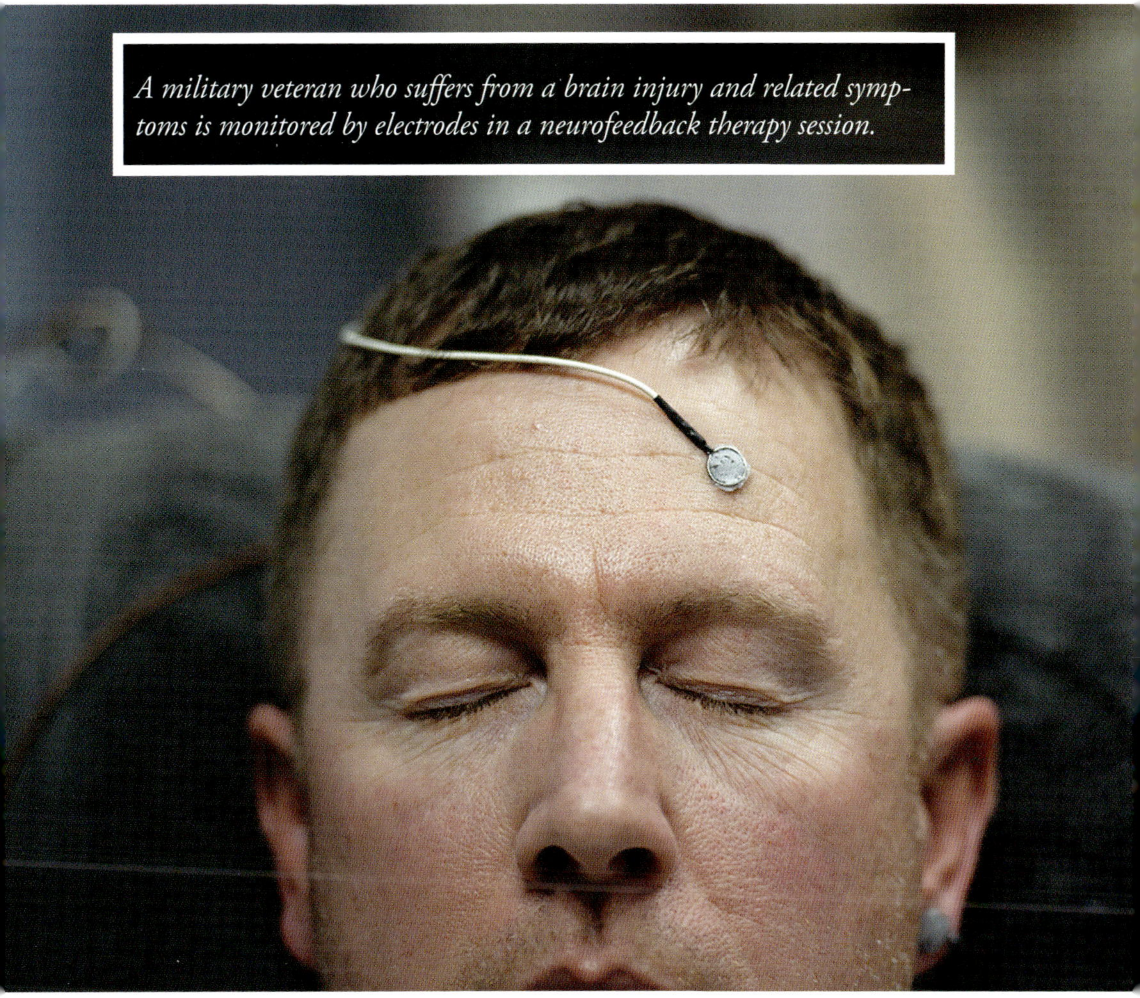

A military veteran who suffers from a brain injury and related symptoms is monitored by electrodes in a neurofeedback therapy session.

sessions. They formulate programs to help patients modify problematic behavior. In many cases, they collaborate with other mental health professionals on plans of treatment.

A neuropsychologist is a clinical psychology specialist who works specifically with patients whose problems stem from brain-related issues. These include mental disorders as well as behavioral problems, brain diseases, and brain injuries.

Counseling psychologists work with patients to understand and cope with their problems. This work is much like that of mental health counselors, which is discussed in detail later in this resource.

Developmental psychologists in the mental health field analyze the patient's lifetime development. They look for indications of psychological progress.

Social psychologists examine a patient's social interactions with other people. Social interactions can have an important effect on the individual's thought processes and resulting behavior.

Forensic psychologists are assigned by a court or hired by attorneys to examine individuals involved in the judicial system. Patients include people who plead insanity when charged with a criminal offense. They also include subjects in civil and family court cases.

Increasingly, psychologists are employed by schools. This has come about as educators have come to understand the effects of mental health on learning. School psychologists are involved especially in the needs of students who have behavioral problems and learning disabilities. They conduct psychological testing of students.

Psychology is a fast-growing career field. The BLS projects the number of jobs for psychologists will increase at a much higher rate than in other occupational areas. The best opportunities await those who have doctoral degrees and specialize in a particular area of psychology.

EDUCATION, TRAINING, AND CREDENTIALS

Most psychologists hold doctoral degrees. Only a master's degree is needed for certain jobs, particularly those in industrial workplaces. A PhD in psychology focuses on research. Research psychologists work mainly in universities, private

HUNDREDS OF MENTAL DISORDERS

Psychologists, psychiatrists, counselors, social workers, and other professionals work with patients who have a wide range of mental disorders. Some disorders are all too common. They have been well understood and successfully treated or managed by generations of mental health professionals. Others are very rare and are not so easily diagnosed and managed. Some patients' mental conditions are complicated and worsened by ailments that are not directly related. For example, many people who suffer from depressive disorders also have anxiety disorders or problems with substance abuse or both.

The *Diagnostic and Statistical Manual of Mental Disorders* (*DSM*), published by the American Psychiatric Association, identifies more than 450 unique mental disorders. (Some psychiatric professionals question whether certain conditions discussed in the *DSM* would be classified more accurately as neurological, not mental, illnesses.) The most common forms of mental illness in American adults are major depressive disorders and other mood disorders, anxiety disorders (panic, phobias, and so forth), and psychotic disorders (schizophrenia, delusions, hallucinations, and so forth). Students who have mental disorders and are in special education classes experience a very high (37 percent) dropout rate, according to the US Department of Education. Suicidal tendencies are alarmingly widespread among teenagers. A 2014 American Association of Suicidology study rated suicide the third-leading cause of death among Americans ages ten to twenty-four.

While those disorders are sadly common, certain mental conditions are so rare most psychiatrists and psychologists never encounter them. An example is alien hand syndrome. Individuals

(continued on the next page)

(continued from the previous page)

with this syndrome believe one of their hands is a separate (though attached), living, thinking appendage that they cannot control. It frequently acts in conflict with their "normal" hand.

A disorder of particular concern, although rare, is apotemnophilia. A person with this disorder believes a healthy body part needs to be amputated. Disturbingly, most people with apotemnophilia and those close to them do not realize there is a problem until the individual has inflicted serious self-injury.

research institutions, and government departments. Students planning to enter clinical psychology usually work toward a doctor of psychology (PsyD) degree. Those who intend to work in schools typically obtain an advanced degree as an education specialist (EdS). They take courses aligned with education as well as psychology curricula.

Areas of study include therapy and counseling, which involve the principles and procedures for diagnosing and treating mental disorders. Students are trained in personal needs assessment and service. They also learn federal and state laws and regulations that govern health care systems and services.

Either before or after earning their doctorates, students in most branches of psychology must obtain one or more years of supervised experience before they can be licensed and enter practice. This experience includes an internship in a professional setting. Specific internship requirements vary in different states. Clinical and counseling psychologists who practice independently must pass the Examination for Professional Practice in Psychology and obtain a state license.

College graduates who have only a bachelor's degree in psychology usually enter fields such as business management or education. Some, though, enter mental health care, beginning their careers as assistants to psychologists or other professionals.

A psychology student in a laboratory exercise is coaching the behavior of a rat. Behavioral studies are a major part of college psychology programs.

PERSONAL QUALITIES

Most of the information about patients is processed and output using computers. Psychologists use not only medical software but also statistical and business applications.

Psychologists desire to counsel and help individuals with mental disorders. They must have excellent people skills, including patience and trustworthiness and the ability to listen to patients and communicate effectively. They must have keen observational instincts and insight to understand patients' reactions. They are inquisitive and eager to investigate complex situations, and they learn to analyze different factors and to identify and solve problems. Patient interactions and workloads are sometimes stressful, and psychologists must be able to manage them smoothly while keeping their emotions under control.

Technology skills will be indispensable in practice. Psychologists commonly use medical software for procedure coding and case management, scientific software for statistical analysis and testing, spreadsheet software for mathematical calculations, accounting software for billing and other business management functions, and standard office program suites.

chapter 3

Mental Health Counselors

Mental health counselors and therapists meet with patients, asking questions and listening carefully as the patients describe their experiences and feelings. Much of their work focuses on preventing problems that can arise as a result of mental disorders. For example, they are trained to observe patients for suicidal tendencies. Job titles may vary; some mental health counselors are called behavior analysts or mental health therapists, specialists, or clinicians.

Counselors develop strategies for helping patients overcome or at least manage depression, stress, anxiety, grief, suicidal thoughts, and other emotional symptoms of their disorders and address relationship problems. For problems that cannot be completely remedied, effective management strategies and activities can reduce the negative impacts. Family members and groups of patients often are included in counseling.

Counselors can connect patients with treatment centers, support groups, and other valuable community services and resources. Typically, counselors collaborate with psychiatrists, psychologists, social workers, and other mental health professionals.

Mental health counselors frequently use cognitive behavioral therapy. This treatment is intended to help their clients

In this exercise, a woman who has anorexia guessed her waist size and then measured it. The activity helped her understand her perception of herself versus reality.

recognize and understand harmful thoughts, attitudes, and behaviors and to introduce positive thoughts instead, resulting in improved behavior.

Some mental health counselors have private practices. Others are affiliated with mental or medical institutions. Some are engaged in workplaces under employee assistance programs provided by employers to serve workers who have mental or emotional difficulties. Most work full time.

Those in private practice must have business training and organizational skills. They must market their services, balance budgets, and collect payment from clients or the clients' insurance companies. Short-distance travel may be required to meet with private patients, and they may schedule consultations after hours and on weekends.

Jobs in mental health counseling are expected to increase more markedly than jobs in most career fields. One reason is that more health insurance policies today include coverage for mental health treatment.

Another is that military combat veterans increasingly seek mental health counseling. As in other careers in mental health, job opportunities usually are greatest in geographical areas that are comparatively underserved by health professionals, such as rural communities.

EDUCATION, TRAINING, AND CREDENTIALS

Mental health counselors study psychology and other aspects of human behavior, sociology and anthropology (ethnic, cultural, and other forms of group behavior), as well as counseling and therapy principles, methods, and treatment. They also are taught personal and client service assessment, standards, and processes.

About two-thirds of mental health counselors have master's degrees. A small percentage hold PhDs, MDs, or other advanced degrees. Master's degrees normally are in psychology, clinical mental health counseling, or a similar area of

This counselor is involved in a group therapy session. Counselors master other forms of therapy, including family therapy and psychotherapy.

mental health. For admission into a master's program, bachelor's degrees in a variety of subjects may be acceptable, including some that are not directly related to mental health.

After completing the master's degree program, an aspiring counselor must work from two thousand to four thousand hours in a clinical setting under the supervision of a licensed professional. This time is similar to a medical student's internship or residency period. Here, the person develops knowledge and skills in different types of therapy, including psychotherapy and group and family therapy. Mental health counseling applicants then must pass an examination and be licensed by the regulating board in their state. Once they begin practice, they are required to take a stipulated number of continuing education classes annually.

Sample State Licensing Requirements

Licensure boards for each state stipulate different requirements for mental health counselor licensing. The requirements in many states are similar, while those in others are notably different.

To receive a mental health counselor license in Florida, an applicant must have at least a master's degree. The degree program must consist of at least sixty semester hours or eighty quarter hours of instruction. Course content includes counseling theories and practice; human growth and development; diagnosis and treatment of psychopathology; human sexuality; group theories and practice; individual evaluation and assessment; career and lifestyle assessment; research and program evaluation; social and cultural foundations; counseling in community settings; substance abuse;

legal, ethical, and professional standards issues; human immunodeficiency virus (HIV) and acquired immune deficiency syndrome (AIDS); and domestic violence.

A Florida applicant needs extensive supervised experience. This training includes at least one thousand hours of clinical internship, practicum, or field experience. In addition, the applicant must have two years of post-degree experience supervised by a licensed mental health counselor. This education consists of at least fifteen hundred hours "providing psychotherapy face-to-face with clients."

The state of Utah requires that a licensure candidate have completed an itemized number of study credits. Established minimum semester or quarter hours must be completed in each of these course areas: professional orientation and ethical practice; social and cultural diversity; group work; human growth and development across the life span; career development; substance use disorders or addictive or compulsive behaviors; psychometric test and measurement theory; research and evaluation in clinical mental health counseling; assessment of mental status; and helping relationships, including theory and skills in counseling and psychotherapy with individuals, couples, or families. Also required are additional courses "related to the practice of counseling."

Applicants in Utah must have finished a minimum of four semesters or six quarter hours in an internship or practicum, "which includes at least 1,000 clock hours of supervised experience, of which at least 400 must be in the provision of mental health therapy."

Some counseling jobs provide on-the-job training for new hires, but most employees consider only applicants who already have some level of experience. Some jobs require five or more years of prior experience.

PERSONAL QUALITIES

Compassion for individuals in stressful situations is the first requirement for mental health counselors. They themselves must be able to keep their composure when patients' tempers and emotions are strained.

Counselors need excellent interpersonal skills to relate to clients with various problems who come from widely different backgrounds. They must be good communicators—patient, noninterrupting listeners as well as effective speakers who can explain ideas clearly to clients. Counselors are especially perceptive, able to understand their clients' worries, statements, subtle meanings, and reactions to suggestions. They can analyze both vulnerabilities and strong points in patients and assemble seemingly unrelated details to find the best solutions to problems.

Mental health counselors must secure their patients' trust because of the need for patients to discuss inner feelings and sensitivities that may be painful to

A counselor listens closely to a patient describing her emotions and concerns. Professional counselors take careful notes to help them monitor patients' progress.

talk about. They gather details and counsel their clients about sensitive personal matters. Counselors make careful notes and keep records. This information must be kept confidential to protect each patient's privacy.

Whether in private or institutional practice, counselors must have at least moderate computer skills. They must be familiar with online research techniques and the use of medical database systems that contain patient information. They communicate frequently by email in their work and commonly use office suite software, including word processors and spreadsheet programs.

chapter 4

SOCIAL WORKERS

In general, the objective of social workers is to identify particular categories of people who have recurring problems that impair their lives and to help them manage or resolve those problems. Clinical social workers diagnose and help treat clients with mental, behavioral, and emotional issues. Their work often includes counseling family members to help them recognize contributing factors to problem situations so they can better support their loved ones.

Clinical social workers who are trained in mental health care assist clients who have mental illnesses and their families. These social workers provide psychotherapy as well as information about available services. They formulate programs of treatment and assistance, usually working with doctors and other mental health professionals.

Mental health social workers sometimes are called on to respond to emergency situations. Over time, they monitor the services and care their clients are receiving in an effort to ensure living improvements. Treatment plans may be altered, depending on how a client is responding.

Besides helping individuals and groups work through their problems, social workers advocate for improved living conditions that could reduce the likelihood of those problems occurring. They make presentations to community groups and to municipal, state, and national government bodies and policy makers.

A social worker accompanies a client who is attempting to serve court documents that grant her permission to visit her children.

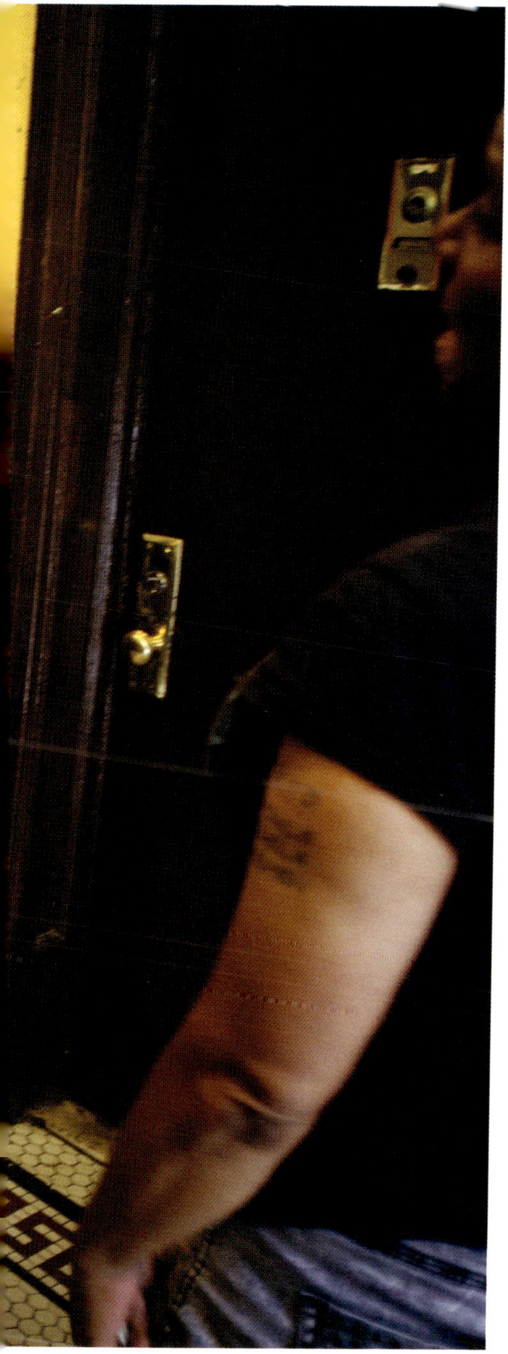

Like mental health counselors, many social workers involved in this field operate their own practices. If so, they must be able to manage common business procedures, such as record keeping and client billing. About half work for local and state government agencies. Others work in group practices that may include mental health professionals with various training and credentials. Most work full time. They sometimes see clients and attend meetings after hours.

A modern trend in social work is distance counseling. Modern technology, including videoconferencing, enables social workers to meet in real time with clients and support groups located many miles away. This approach is convenient especially in health care programs serving less-populated communities.

The job future for clinical social workers is good, although demands vary by specialty. About 18 percent of all social workers practice in the areas of mental health and substance

A Challenging Concentration in Social Work

Mental health social workers provide more than half of the mental health services in the United States, according to administrators in the University of Southern California School of Social Work's mental health concentration. They work in all categories of mental health settings.

"Social workers treat all kinds of situations and all levels of care," explains Shannon Mayeda, clinical associate professor in the program. "We work with a variety of issues. We treat people with grief and loss and adjustment. We work with people who have severe and persistent mental illnesses, such as schizophrenia and bipolar disorder. We also treat people with addictions."

Students who enroll in the concentration are exposed to individual treatment, group treatment, and family-based treatment methods. They learn about assessment, diagnosis, the course of illnesses, and treatment options. They come to understand why people behave as they do and the factors that impact their behavior—the homes and communities they live in as well as their workplaces.

"We deal with theory, and then we deal with practice," Mayeda says. "Once we understand what kind of symptoms we're working with in the individual, now what do we do about it?"

In addition to classroom studies, students gain firsthand experience in the community. Field placements are part of the program, supervised by veteran social workers.

Clinical associate professor Betsy Phillips finds the mental health concentration a particularly stimulating career field. "If you are a person who likes one-on-one interaction, you love talking to people about issues and their problems and how people can feel better, and you just like connecting with people in an interpersonal way, that's what I was drawn to mental health for, because I just loved finding out what makes people tick."

Phillips observes that many mental health social workers today choose to work in schools. "There's such a need for people who are comfortable and experienced and trained working with children who have been traumatized."

abuse combined, according to the BLS. Job growth in those specialty areas is expected to accelerate faster than in many other social work categories. Those with master's degrees have the most job opportunities.

Members of a community assistance team talk with a homeless woman. Case workers help homeless people, especially those with health issues, find stable living situations.

EDUCATION, TRAINING, AND CREDENTIALS

A bachelor's degree in social work or a related field is required to begin a social work career. Those with bachelor's degrees can find jobs as mental health assistants or caseworkers, supervised by licensed social workers. Clinical social workers must have a master's degree and two or more years of experience working under the supervision of a clinical professional.

Courses in bachelor's degree studies generally include psychology, sociology, anthropology, counseling, and therapy. Students learn the principles of providing client service. English courses hone composition, grammar, and spelling skills.

To enter a master's degree program, students may obtain a bachelor's degree in social work (BSW) or a subject such as psychology or sociology. Master's degree programs usually take two years but may take as little as one year. During graduate school, students participate in internships or practicums, gaining field experience.

All clinical social workers and most nonclinical workers must obtain state licenses. Some acquire further education for certification in specialty areas. A minority eventually obtain doctoral degrees and teach in college and university social work programs.

Many college students who major in social work are not sure at the outset which category of clients they want to help. Those who continue in master's degree programs usually commit to a particular practice area such as geriatric, adolescent, or mental health social work.

PERSONAL QUALITIES

Most important, social workers must have compassion for people with difficult and often complex problems. They need

A social worker interviews a geriatric patient in a relaxed setting. Geriatrics is one of many specialty areas of social work.

excellent communication and interpersonal skills to develop effective relationships with clients and fully understand the issues with which they are coping. Social workers must be able to correctly assess problems and their contributing factors and to arrive at practical solutions.

In the course of their daily work, social workers interact closely not only with clients and client groups but also with supervisors and colleagues. They must be well organized. They see many patients most days and document details of each visit. Good time management skills are essential.

Social workers must have sincere compassion for their patients, as shown here by a professional consoling a young woman under stress.

Because social work often involves clients who are living in stressful circumstances, these professionals must be able to diffuse hot-tempered outbursts. Social workers must be calm, objective, and positive in volatile encounters.

Aspiring social workers cannot neglect developing technology skills for their jobs. Like most medical professionals, clinical social workers use computers in their daily routines. Much, if not most, of the information they gather and file is in electronic rather than written form. Besides word processing and email programs, their work may involve desktop publishing software for preparing informational materials, forms, and reports and presentation software to illustrate oral presentations to client, professional, and civic groups. They frequently conduct internet research and access medical record databases.

chapter 5

Counselors in Behavioral Disorders and Rehabilitation

The overall objective of behavioral disorder counselors is to help their clients improve personal relationships. This goal is an important part of treatment for persons with mental disorders.

Rehabilitation counselors in the mental health field endeavor to help patients live independently. The turmoil and trauma brought about by a mental illness often result in temporary commitment to an institution. With effective rehabilitation, they can return to productive, enjoyable lives in the community.

These professionals work in mental health facilities, community health centers, private practices, and sometimes in other settings, such as prisons. They generally work full-time schedules and may have to work evenings and weekends.

Behavioral Disorder Counselors

Behavioral disorder counselors study and document a patient's mental health and physical health history as well as the person's physical condition and unusual behavior patterns. They detect circumstances or habits that would thwart successful treatment. They determine when treatment is appropriate and help establish goals. Treatment plans typically are discussed with the patient's family members to inform them and engage their support.

A counselor comforts an inmate in a prison program intended to help combat addiction and transition imprisoned addicts back into the community.

In certain cases, courts assign counselors to intervene in crises involving mental health patients. Some counseling sessions are conducted with groups of patients. Invariably, clients learn to manage stress related to their problems.

The ultimate goal of a treatment process is to help the person change behavior patterns and, if possible, recover. Toward that end, the counselor may find outside support groups, community outreach programs, job services, and other resources for the patient and family. Counselors or other advisers often help patients find jobs or return to interrupted careers. They also help clients build confidence in their relationships with others.

Patients in a rehabilitation program share their experiences with one another and with their counselor. Counselors sometimes work with individuals, sometimes with groups.

Behavioral disorder counselors may have private practices, either solo or with other counselors and related professionals. These private practices function as businesses and must be run efficiently. Others are employed at mental health facilities, community health centers, and prisons. There, they usually work with teams of professionals who include medical doctors, psychiatrists, social workers, and others. Most behavioral disorder counselors work full time.

The role of behavioral disorder counselor is one of the fastest-growing job categories in mental health, according to the BLS. Increased insurance coverage of mental health issues is expanding the number of patients admitted to treatment and prevention facilities.

Rehabilitation Counselors

Medical rehabilitation is the process of restoring a sick or injured patient to good health or returning the person to the best level of health possible. Rehabilitation counselors in the mental health field work with patients to help them cope with and manage the negative effects of their disorders. The objective is to enable them to return to an independent lifestyle and resume their careers and normal activities. In many cases, rehabilitation takes months or years. During this time, the counselor keeps careful notes, monitoring patients' progress.

Rehab counselors evaluate each patient's overall health, capabilities, skills, experiences, and interests. They work to help them manage their disabilities, often by recognizing limitations and making adjustments in the way they do things. They help patients acquire any needed resources. The treatment plans they follow usually are developed with other mental health professionals.

Part of their work is done with people with whom the patient associates. For example, they may help find employment and

Much of the dialogue between patients and rehabilitation counselors is exciting and enjoyable as the client discusses personal interests and together they consider potential employment opportunities.

job training. This assistance often involves explaining to employers any special needs that the patient may have and state and federal disability laws. In this situation, the counselor assumes the role of advocate.

Like behavioral disorder counselors, some rehab counselors maintain private practices. Others are on staff at facilities where mental health patients are treated.

Job growth for rehabilitation counselors will not be as vigorous as for behavioral disorder counselors, the BLS predicts. However, it will be more energetic than the average growth rate in all career fields.

Education, Training, and Credentials

For behavioral disorder counselors, a wide range of job definitions calls for employees with varying levels of education. At least a bachelor's degree is required for most jobs. Some counselors have master's degrees; certain jobs require only a high school diploma with appropriate certification. Counselors who have more training can provide more services and need less supervision.

Behavioral disorder counselors have studied psychology, counseling, therapy, anthropology, sociology, and related subjects. They also are trained in customer service and have a solid educational foundation in English usage.

Rehabilitation counselors usually have master's degrees. Academic subjects include psychology, therapy, counseling, and client service. Students learn theories as well as techniques for providing effective rehabilitation for mental health patients. A major objective is successful job placement for their clients. For this, counselors need to be familiar with education and training systems and programs.

State licensing is required for behavioral disorder counselors who enter private practice. They must have master's degrees

What Employers Expect

Counseling jobs in the mental health field differ greatly. Duties depend on the setting and the clientele of the employing organization. Educational and licensing requirements vary. Although most jobs are full time, part-time opportunities are available. Here are the basic job functions and requirements described in two actual employment advertisements.

Behavioral Health Counselor. A hospital in New Hampshire seeks a professional for behavioral health counseling and for assessing and diagnosing mental disorders. Much of the counseling and treatment is with children as young as age four, making behavioral health assessments and working with a treatment team. Patients are of different personalities, cultures, and backgrounds. A calm, reassuring demeanor is needed for stressful situations. The counselor must be a good communicator, well organized, knowledgeable about available behavioral health resources, and computer competent. Confidential handling of sensitive information is essential. Licensing as an independent clinical social worker is required, with at least three to five years of independent counseling experience. Certification in specialty areas such as grief or substance abuse is preferred. The job involves day shifts, thirty-two hours a week.

Rehabilitation Counselor, Mental Health Services. A community-based, nonprofit health association in New York needs a rehabilitation counselor to work in treatment apartments with adults who are recovering from mental illnesses. Through therapy, crisis management, skill development, and other forms of support, the counselor will help residents achieve independent living within the community. The job involves administering medication and transporting clients in an agency car. Compassion, respect, good judgment, multitasking, and the ability to work independently of supervision are vital. The counselor must be computer literate, capable of operating an electronic records database, and have good communication skills. Candidates need a bachelor's degree and at least three years of experience working with adults in mental health. The job requires twenty-five hours a week (classified as part time); some shifts are during evenings and weekends.

and at least two thousand hours of clinical work experience under approved supervision. Those who are not engaged in private practice may or may not need a license or certificate, depending on the state where they work.

For rehab counselors, licensing and certification requirements vary by state. An internship or other program for gaining field experience is necessary for many jobs. Between two thousand and four thousand hours of clinical supervision may be necessary. Licensed counselors must earn continuing education credits throughout their careers.

Personal Qualities

Like mental health counselors, counselors in behavioral disorders and rehabilitation must have compassion for their clients, who often go through prolonged periods of stress and frustration. They must listen carefully and patiently to fully understand a patient's unique problems and how subtle circumstances of life may be affecting the issues. Counselors develop interpersonal skills so that they can relate to and communicate effectively with clients from widely diverse backgrounds. They must be able to clearly explain ideas and information that sometimes are complex. They must cooperate well with other members of evaluation and treatment teams.

Rehabilitation counselors, in particular, need critical thinking and deductive reasoning skills. These traits enable

A counselor and an outreach worker (standing) *learn details of a homeless man's situation, hoping to help him find good housing and other needed services.*

them to formulate good treatment plans and keep them on track. Behavioral disorder counselors are more likely to encounter patients at highly stressful moments, and they have to be able to cope with volatile situations. All counselors must be able to prioritize, plan, and organize their tasks efficiently. Counselors write reports and work with other mental health professionals in evaluating clients' needs and progress and developing assistance plans.

Counselors need computer skills for their interactions with patients and colleagues. They access and compile medical information from both online and offline sources, work with medical case management software, communicate by email and videoconferencing, and conduct research via the internet.

chapter 6

Psychiatric Technicians and Aides

Technicians and aides who work in this field of health care provide ongoing therapeutic care and monitoring of mental patients and persons with emotional and developmental challenges. They help patients perform daily activities and maintain sanitary, safe living conditions. Technicians and aides work under psychiatrists' supervision as members of a team that generally includes psychologists, therapists, and social workers. They work in psychiatric and residential or outpatient treatment centers or in hospitals specializing in mental health.

The needs of patients vary widely. Some require intensive, long-term care as a result of major developmental problems. Others need relatively short-term rehabilitation.

Psychiatric (mental health) technicians work through scheduled therapy with each patient and record progress. They observe the patient's actions, keep regular health records (blood pressure, weight, temperature, and so forth), discuss concerns with clients and other staff members, administer medicine as prescribed by doctors, and help the client with therapy and recreation. They usually are involved in the process of admitting clients to and discharging them from health care facilities. Both technicians and aides may be needed to help a patient with eating, bathing, and other routine activities and to control violent behavior.

Psychiatric aides or orderlies help patients perform ordinary activities (such as bathing, dressing, and eating) each day. They make sure bed linens are fresh and handle other home care and hygienic tasks to keep the living environment clean and safe. Aides drive or accompany patients on errands, visits to clinical appointments, field trips, and entertainment events. They help patients participate in challenging learning endeavors and hobbies.

Technicians and aides working in mental health care have more frequent daily interactions with patients than most other professionals on the treatment team. For this reason, they can have a uniquely valuable impact on the client's attitude and life.

Both full-time and part-time jobs are available for psychiatric technicians and aides. Shifts are staffed around the clock at residential treatment centers and hospitals. This schedule means technicians and aides may be assigned evening, weekend, and holiday hours.

Proper nutrition and daily care are important in treating psychiatric patients. Here, a psychiatric aide helps a patient with eating her meal.

The BLS projects that job growth for technicians and aides will be approximately the same as the average growth rate for all career fields. There has been a shifting trend in job settings as a result of the United States' increased aging population. Dementia, Alzheimer's disease, and similar mental disorders are more common among the elderly. Many of those individuals live in residential care facilities, which thus have a rising need for aides and technicians.

EDUCATION, TRAINING, AND CREDENTIALS

Most jobs for psychiatric aides call for only a high school diploma. Technicians need postsecondary training such as nursing courses. Certification is required for some technician jobs. Students who want to become mental health technicians may consider enrolling in a technical school or community college program to obtain an associate's degree in psychiatric technology. They study psychology and counseling as well as biology and related sciences. Technicians may be licensed practical nurses or nursing assistants; this background gives them clinical experience, which is necessary in many work environments.

Mental health technicians and aides in institutions frequently must support patients who have mobility difficulties. Workers must be in good physical condition to perform these duties.

Some jobs require prior on-the-job training; many employers provide their own

Skyla Jefferson
1548 Federal Street • Webster, WI 65000
Home: (006) 321-3456; Mobile: (006) 876-2345 • tsjeff@sub80x4.com

IMMEDIATE OBJECTIVE:
To obtain a part-time or volunteer position as a health care aide, preferably in a facility for mental health patients. I want to learn everything I can about caring for people with mental disorders and challenges.

LONG-TERM OBJECTIVE:
A career in mental health service. Eventually, I want to earn a master's degree to become a clinical psychiatric counselor.

EDUCATION
East Webster High School, Class of 2019 (3.1 GPA).

WORK EXPERIENCE
• 2016–Present: Counter staffer at Time-In, a local short-order restaurant. Duties include taking customer orders and cleaning the dining area. Work includes constant interaction with customers and other workers.
• 2017–Present: Volunteer at Hope Retreat, a local shelter for the homeless. Duties include meal service and janitorial tasks on weekends.

• School Year 2016–2017: Reporter for high school newspaper. Articles include profile interviews with Darla Anders, school mental health counselor, and William Fletcher, psychology teacher. I also wrote an in-depth feature about the homeless shelter where I volunteer part time.

SPECIAL SKILLS AND KNOWLEDGE
• Spanish fluency
• Avid reader of mental health publications, including *Better Mental Health*, *MyHealth*, *Psychology Today*, and *Women's Health*
• Proficiency in numerous computer programs and apps, including Microsoft Word, PowerPoint, Excel, OneNote, Outlook, and Access

FAVORITE ACTIVITIES
• Camping and entertainment outings with family, friends, and church groups
• Reading, chess, word puzzles
• Involvement in school fund-raising drives

REFERENCES
• Darla Anders, mental health counselor, East Webster High School; school phone (006) 321-3333
• William Fletcher, psychology teacher, East Webster High School; school phone (006) 321-3333
• Rosemary Flynn, director, Hope Retreat, Webster; office phone (006) 321-9988

This sample résumé for a mental health care aide is neat and professional looking. It has an easy-to-read format that makes it simple for an interviewer to find relevant information.

training. Some job training is needed before a technician or aide can begin duties unsupervised. Training is provided by experienced technicians and aides. It may take only a few months or as long as a year or two.

Technicians and aides must have a working knowledge of public safety and security standards and practices. They need to be familiar with security systems, safety equipment, and injury prevention measures. Part of their job is to protect their clients and associates as well as physical property and stored records.

Psychiatric aides are not licensed. Only a few states require licensing for psychiatric technicians. Licensure in those states requires completion of an education program and an examination. The American Association of Psychiatric Technicians issues licenses for different competency levels.

Psychiatric technicians and aides can improve their future job prospects with ongoing training. Workshops that focus on specific aspects of their job

Two psychiatric aides compare notes at their station. Computer skills are necessary to link patient information between desktop and mobile devices.

periodically are available at health facilities and community colleges. Workers also can attend lectures and receive in-service instruction.

PERSONAL QUALITIES

Technicians and aides, like all professionals who work in mental health, must be compassionate and patient. They must genuinely care about their clients' well-being and maintain a good rapport with each client. Patients often can be unpleasant and even violent. Technicians and aides must have a calming influence when patients are under stress. They must be quickly adaptable, able to assess unexpected situations as they arise each day, make sound decisions, and solve problems. Workers must have good interpersonal, observational, and communication skills to enable them to understand clients' questions and needs, to perceive behavioral changes, and to detect discomforts or potential emerging problems. They offer a sympathetic ear to patients' complaints and provide emotional support.

Both technicians and aides—aides in particular—must be in good physical condition because they frequently are needed to move medical equipment and furniture and to help patients with physical activities. Patients sometimes have to be restrained. Much of the work of technicians and aides is done on their feet. Injury rates are significantly high among medical aides and technicians.

Some technology skills are needed. Both aides and technicians routinely use word processing, electronic mail, and spreadsheet programs. Aides may be required to enter and retrieve data in computer systems. Technicians use medical-specific software and may be required to process inventory management records. Technicians and aides use medical diagnostic instruments and therapeutic equipment.

chapter 7

Related Careers

Many career seekers eventually find their way into mental health care service after working in jobs that are not linked directly to mental health. After seeing firsthand the needs of mental health patients and realizing the impact they can make in those individuals' lives, some of these people acquire the educational credentials needed for a career in applied mental health care.

Related vocations include those of physician assistants, registered nurses, and nursing assistants and orderlies. Others involve administrative work performed by people such as social and human service assistants and social and community service managers.

Physician Assistants

Physician assistants (PAs) are members of medical teams who examine and diagnose patients and help with treatment. They work with a supervising doctor and with nurses and other medical professionals.

Some of their duties overlap with those of doctors and registered nurses. Besides examining patients and reviewing their medical histories, PAs are trained to diagnose illnesses, order and analyze blood tests and other diagnostic tests, and prescribe medication based on research of different treatments. They evaluate and keep records of patients' progress. They also are

A physician assistant provides information to a patient. Educating patients is an important aspect of the work in mental health careers.

engaged in education. They provide information not only to patients and their families directly but also to groups of individuals enrolled in outreach programs.

Most physician assistants work full time in doctors' offices or hospitals. Those who work in hospitals may be assigned evening and weekend shifts. They may be on call to respond to situations after hours.

Physician assistants usually need a master's degree with a focus in science. Classroom and lab study are required in subjects such as pathology, physiology, anatomy, pharmacology, clinical medicine, and physical diagnosis. Students undergo supervised clinical training. Some PA students are experienced registered nurses or emergency medical technicians.

PAs must be licensed. They take an examination prepared by the National Commission on Certification of Physician Assistants. They also must complete one hundred hours of continuing education every two years.

Necessary personal traits of a PA include problem-solving and communication skills, compassion, emotional stability, and attention to detail. PAs must be in good physical condition because much of their work is done on their feet.

The job market for physician assistants is growing much more rapidly than those for most other careers, according to the BLS. One reason is that they can perform many of the same functions as doctors, at less cost.

Registered Nurses

Registered nurses set up and coordinate plans of care, working closely with doctors and other medical professionals. They keep patients informed, answer questions and advise them, and support them and their families emotionally. RNs keep records of patients' medical histories and update the records based on observations. They are involved in administering medicine and other forms of treatment, performing and analyzing diagnostic tests, and educating patients and families in how to manage the disorder.

Many RNs who work specifically with mental health patients are clinical nurse specialists, a category of advanced-practice registered nurses. They work with other mental health professionals and usually assume leadership roles, supervising staffers such as nursing assistants and home health aides.

Most registered nurses work in hospitals or treatment centers. Others work in physicians' offices and for home health care firms. They typically work in shifts and may be on call at night and on weekends.

A doctor and nurse examine patient details on a laptop computer in the patient's hospital room. Registered nurses typically work in institutional environments.

To become a registered nurse, a student must obtain a bachelor of science degree in nursing (BSN), associate's degree in nursing, or diploma from a credentialed nursing program. Degree programs include science courses, specifically anatomy, chemistry, physiology, microbiology, and nutrition. Nursing students also take psychology and classes in behavioral science, communication, critical thinking, and leadership.

Bachelor of science programs usually take four years to complete. Associate's degree programs take two to three years. Many nurses with associate's degrees or nursing program diplomas eventually return to school to earn a BSN, which opens up more job opportunities for them. Clinical nurse specialists require a master's degree.

Licensing is required before entering registered nursing practice. Applicants must pass the National Council Licensure Examination. Clinical nurse specialists must obtain additional licensing.

Important characteristics of registered nurses include communication and critical-thinking skills, compassion, emotional stability, and good physical stamina. They must be good organizers with an eye for details.

The demand for registered nurses is growing much faster than the job growth rate for most other occupations, according to the BLS. Higher levels of education generally are required for the most advanced jobs.

NURSING ASSISTANTS AND ORDERLIES

Nursing assistants, or aides, provide basic daily care for patients in hospitals and residential care facilities, such as mental health institutions. They help patients toilet, bathe, dress, and eat. For patients who have trouble moving, aides help them turn in their beds and transfer them from bed to chair or wheelchair. They regularly check temperature and blood pressure and report to nurses if a patient expresses a particular discomfort or worry. In some states, nursing assistants can obtain special certification to administer medicines.

Orderlies move patients around in wheelchairs, change bed linens, keep supply cabinets and drawers adequately stocked, and clean the facilities. Although they are not as highly trained or educated as others on a mental health team, nursing assistants and orderlies generally spend the most time with patients under long-term care. They become the main caregivers. They are supervised by registered nurses or licensed practical nurses.

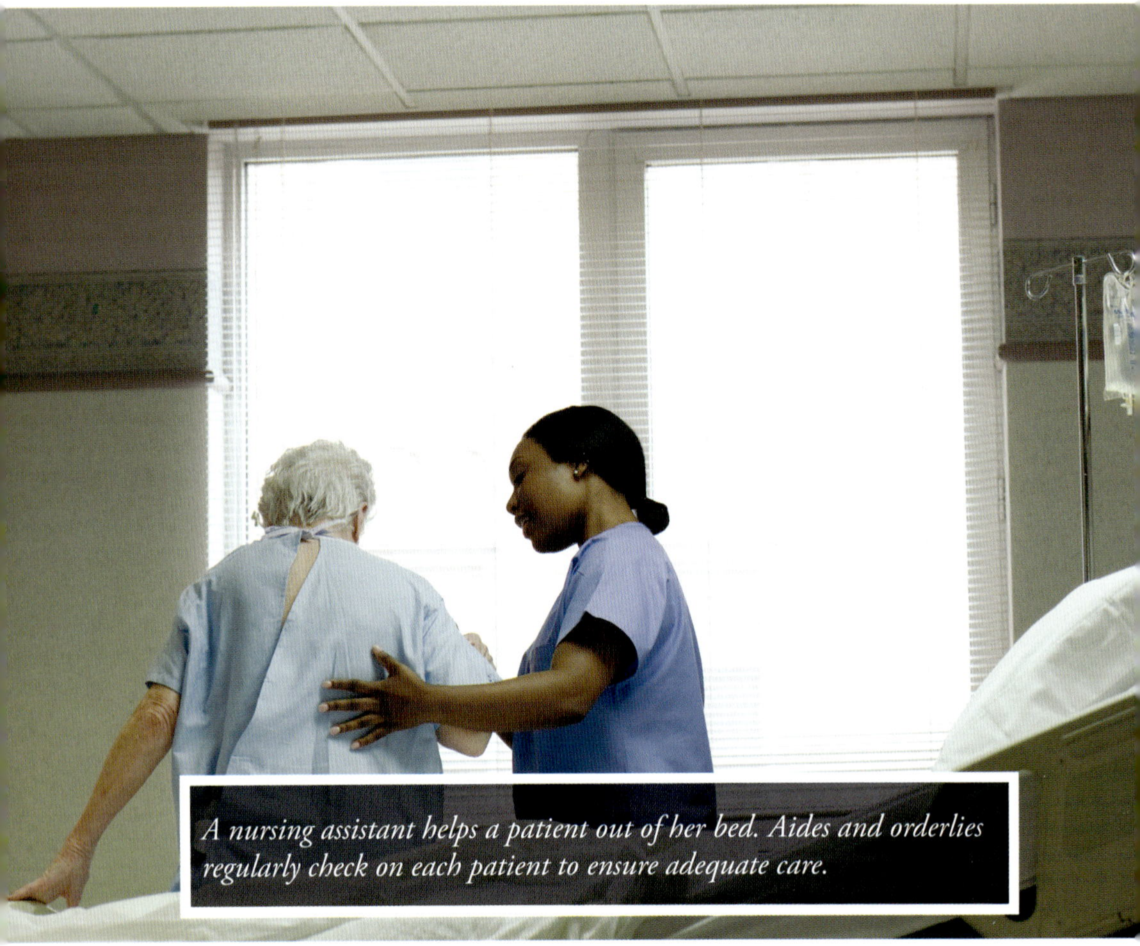

A nursing assistant helps a patient out of her bed. Aides and orderlies regularly check on each patient to ensure adequate care.

Most nursing assistants and orderlies work at skilled nursing facilities, hospitals, and continuing care communities. They generally work full time on assigned shifts, which may include night and weekend shifts.

Nursing assistants are required to complete a state-approved training program, perform supervised clinical work, and pass a competency exam to become registered. Training programs teach them basic nursing principles. Some approved programs are offered in high schools. Others are available at community and technical colleges and through hospital training departments.

A high school diploma is required for most jobs as orderlies. New employees are given on-the-job training. In many workplaces, orderlies must be trained in cardiopulmonary resuscitation and basic life support.

Aides and orderlies need good communication skills to understand patients' concerns and pass them along to nurses and other professionals. They must be patient and compassionate with those they care for. Because much of their job calls for lifting or assisting patients physically, aides and orderlies must be able to perform strenuous work. They experience a higher rate of injuries than most others in mental health careers. To reduce the risk, they commonly wear support belts and braces.

Like many other health care jobs, those for nursing assistants and orderlies are expected to increase dramatically, according to the BLS. The job market may be somewhat volatile in health care facilities that rely on government funding. BLS statisticians note that turnover is high in this job category because of stress, physical requirements, and comparatively low pay.

Social and Human Service Assistants

Social and human service assistants work with clients and their families to help the clients reside at home and care for themselves or to find assistance with daily needs if necessary. In the area of mental health, they connect people who have disorders with support groups and self-help organizations and help them locate other useful resources. For people with severe mental disorders, they may be able to arrange group housing where the individuals can take care of themselves and cope with their illness.

These workers often assist social workers and other mental health professionals in determining what clients need

SOCIAL AND COMMUNITY SERVICE MANAGERS

Some mental health jobs are administrative. Social and community service managers supervise community organizations and social service programs that serve certain groups of people. Organizations may benefit the mentally ill, the homeless, the elderly, or the unemployed, for example. Managers handle budgets and administrative details, hire and train staff, collect data to measure the effectiveness of the program, meet with fund-raisers, look for program improvements, and make presentations to make the public aware of the program and its benefits.

Service programs and organizations may be operated by family service groups, state or local government agencies, religious or civic organizations, or residential care facilities. Many are nonprofit; some are run by for-profit companies. Those that serve the mentally ill are staffed by social workers, counselors, and other trained professionals. Most managers work full time; overtime may be required during certain periods.

Social and community service managers have at least a bachelor's degree in such subjects as social work, public health, business administration, or urban studies. Some organizations prefer that managers have master's degrees and significant experience in a related field. Many managers are former social workers.

Personal qualities considered vital for these administrative jobs include managerial and time management skills as well as analytical and problem-solving skills. Managers must be able to communicate and interact with others effectively.

The BLS projects that the number of these types of management jobs will grow somewhat faster than the overall job growth average. The job market may be affected by local and state government budget streamlining.

and finding benefits and community services for them. They help clients fill out necessary paperwork when applying for assistance. They transport their clients around the community. Assistants also monitor their clients' well-being and make sure they are receiving appropriate help.

Social and human service assistants typically work with either for-profit or nonprofit social service organizations, local and state agencies, and residential care facilities. Much of their work involves travel throughout the community. Some of the work is done in doctors' offices, hospitals, clinics, and shelters. Most workers are full time; some of their work may be done on nights and weekends.

Practically all social and human service assistants have at least a high school diploma and receive on-the-job training. Some jobs require additional education, such as either an associate's degree in behavioral science or a certificate or both, and prior experience. Some employers consider experience more important than a college degree, although higher education usually is necessary for advancement. Workers with a high school diploma and no experience typically perform routine work. Those with college credits may find jobs as program coordinators or group home managers. Many assistants eventually obtain bachelor's or master's degrees to become social workers or counselors.

Social and human service assistants must be good at communication, organization, problem solving, and time management. They must have compassion for their clients and possess interpersonal skills to put their clients at ease.

The BLS projects job growth for social and human service assistants will be faster than the average for all occupations. Opportunities are best for applicants with a college degree. Turnover is fairly high because of modest salaries and sometimes heavy workloads.

MANY OPPORTUNITIES TO SERVE

Like many other service professions, mental health service involves teamwork. Not all jobs require medical training, although most require some degree of understanding of the clinical problems that confront the people who are served by the profession. Together, these dedicated workers make conditions more enjoyable and productive for patients.

Different careers in mental health call for different aptitudes and skill sets. One personal trait is common throughout the profession: a sense of compassion for those with mental disorders, leading to a desire to help them establish better lives.

glossary

advocate One who defends or pleads the cause of another.
amnesia Loss of memory.
appendage Part of the body (finger, arm, foot) that projects outward.
biochemical Related to chemicals or chemical processes in living bodies.
chronic Having an illness that goes on for a long time.
civil court A court that deals with cases involving private rather than criminal legal conflicts.
clinical Based on observation of a patient and patient behavior.
cognitive therapy Psychotherapy that attempts to replace negative with positive thoughts.
curriculum Set of study courses with a related theme subject.
diagnostic Related to testing conducted for the purpose of diagnosing a problem.
discipline Practice area such as (in medicine) mental health, elder care, or neurology.
hallucinations Imaginings of things that are not real, caused by nervous disorders or drugs.
hypochondria Obsession with an imaginary ailment.
hysteria Uncontrollable mental excitement.
neurological Related to the nervous system.
osteopathic Related to the field of medicine that focuses on the treatment of medical conditions by manipulating and massaging bones, joints, and muscles and by prescribing medicines, among other types of therapy.
practicum Supervised training in practical applications of what students have learned.
psychometric test A scientific test used to identify and measure someone's mental ability and behavioral traits. It

is used to find out how suitable someone is for performing certain tasks.

schizophrenia A serious mental illness in which a person cannot think or behave in a normal manner and may experience delusions.

sedative Medicine that causes a patient to relax or sleep.

straitjacket A garment that holds the arms tight against the body to prevent violent thrashing.

syndrome A set of symptoms that suggests a certain medical disorder.

for more information

American Mental Health Counselors Association (AMHCA)
675 North Washington Street, Suite 470
Alexandria, VA 22314
(703) 548-6002
Website: http://www.amhca.org
Facebook: @amhca
Twitter: @AMHCA1
LinkedIn: @amhca
The primary national organization of licensed clinical mental health counselors offers its members education, advocacy, and leadership and collaboration opportunities.

American Psychiatric Association (APA)
1000 Wilson Boulevard, Suite 1825
Arlington, VA 22209-3901
(888) 357-7924
Website: http://www.psychiatry.org
Facebook: @AmericanPsychiatricAssociation
Twitter: @APAPsychiatric
The APA has more than thirty-seven thousand members in more than one hundred countries. They are involved in psychiatric practice, research, and education.

Bureau of Labor Statistics (BLS)
US Department of Labor
Postal Square Building
2 Massachusetts Avenue NE
Washington, DC 20212-0001
(202) 691-5200
Website: https://www.bls.gov

Facebook: @departmentoflabor
Twitter: @BLS_gov
This US Department of Labor updates statistics on all types of jobs, salaries, growth trends, and other statistics. The BLS publishes the *Occupational Outlook Handbook* (https://www.bls.gov/ooh), which includes career data and information about various jobs, including mental health service jobs.

Canadian Association of Social Workers (CASW)
383 Parkdale Avenue, Suite 402
Ottawa, ON K1Y 4R4
Canada
(613) 729-6668
Website: http://www.casw-acts.ca
Facebook: @Canadian.Association.of.Social.Workers
Twitter: @casw_acts
Canada's association of professional social workers was established to support and strengthen the profession and advance social justice for Canadians.

Canadian Mental Health Association (CMHA)
500-250 Dundas Street West
Toronto, ON M5T 2Z5
Canada
(416) 646-5557
Website: http://www.cmha.ca
Facebook: @CMHANational
Twitter: @CMHA_NTL
YouTube: @cmhanational
The CMHA is a voluntary charity established to help maintain and improve mental health for Canadians. It provides support services and helps individuals access community-based resources.

National Association of Social Workers (NASW)
750 First Street NE, Suite 800
Washington, DC 20002
(202) 408-8600
Website: http://www.socialworkers.org
Facebook: @socialworkers
Twitter: @nasw
This organization of professional US social workers provides current information, research findings, and other resources for its members.

National Institute of Mental Health (NIMH)
6001 Executive Boulevard, Room 6200
Bethesda, MD 20892-9663
(866) 615-6464
Website: http://www.nimh.nih.gov
Facebook: @nimhgov
Twitter: @nimhgov
YouTube: @nimhgov
The NIMH, part of the US Department of Health and Human Services, is the main federal agency for research about mental disorders.

Websites

Because of the changing nature of internet links, Rosen Publishing has developed an online list of websites related to the subject of this book. This site is updated regularly. Please use this link to access the list:

http://www.rosenlinks.com/ECAR/Mental

for further reading

Flath, Camden. *21st-century Counselors: New Approaches to Mental Health & Substance Abuse.* Broomall, PA: Mason Crest Publishers, 2011.

Fontaine, Karen Lee. *Mental Health Nursing.* 6th ed. Upper Saddle River, NJ: Pearson Prentice Hall, 2009.

Kuther, Tara L., and Robert D. Morgan. *Careers in Psychology: Opportunities in a Changing World.* Boston, MA: Wadsworth/Cengage Learning, 2010.

Metz, Kim. *Careers in Mental Health: Opportunities in Psychology, Counseling, and Social Work.* West Sussex, UK: John Wiley & Sons, Ltd., 2016.

Morkes, Andrew. *Hot Health Care Careers: More Than 25 Cutting-Edge Occupations with the Fastest Growth and Most New Positions.* Chicago, IL: College & Career Press, 2011.

National Learning Corporation. *Mental Health Counselor: Test Preparation Study Guide, Questions & Answers.* Syosset, NY: National Learning Corporation, 2015.

Quan, Kathy. *The Everything Guide to Careers in Health Care: Find the Job That's Right for You.* Avon, MA: F&W Publications, Inc., 2007.

Roland, James. *Careers in Mental Health.* San Diego, CA: ReferencePoint Press, 2017.

Salzman, Amy. *A Still Quiet Place for Teens: A Mindfulness Workbook to Ease Stress and Difficult Emotions.* Oakland, CA: Instant Help, 2016.

Sheen, Barbara. *Careers in Health Care.* San Diego, CA: ReferencePoint Press, 2015.

Torrey, Tricia. *So You Want to Be a Patient Advocate? Choosing a Career in Health or Patient Advocacy.* Baldwinsville, NY: DiagKNOWsis Media, 2015.

bibliography

American Association of Suicidology. "U.S.A. Suicide: 2013 Official Final Data." Retrieved March 2017. http://www.suicidology.org/Portals/14/docs/Resources/FactSheets/2013datapgsv2alt.pdf.

American University of Antigua College of Medicine. "Clinical Rotations: What They Are and Why They're Necessary." Retrieved March 2017. http://www.auamed.org/blog/clinical-rotations-theyre-necessary.

CareerOneStop. US Department of Labor. https://www.careerinfonet.org.

Florida Board of Clinical Social Work, Marriage & Family Therapy and Mental Health Counseling. "Licensed Mental Health Counselor." Retrieved March 2017. http://floridasmentalhealthprofessions.gov/licensing/licensed-mental-health-counselor.

Friedman, Michael. "America's Mental Health System Needs Improvement, But Gains of the Past Give Hope for the Future." *Huffington Post*, May 18, 2013. http://www.huffingtonpost.com/michael-friedman-lmsw/mental-health-system_b_2848382.html.

Hussung, Tricia. "5 Rare Mental Disorders You Probably Haven't Heard Of." Concordia University, Saint Paul, October 28, 2015. http://online.csp.edu/blog/psychology/5-rare-mental-disorders.

Indeed. "Rehabilitation Counselor—Mental Health Services—Part-time." Job posting, March 20, 2017. https://www.indeed.com/cmp/MHA-of-Westchester/jobs/Rehabilitation-Counselor-34c48a7c5548545f?sjdu=QwrRXKrqZ3CNX5W-O9jEvYTmEpu6KCkGwIwnxjL7IbKxyXH4akI-Dz6dpJ7XIcHpNivS9b__4hTOAR9Pr6egWe1

x7FneG1yiLK3cLw8GFyZWvb_9FY9WBZko5wRlPRnk U0cKWmhAEzopf3PUWJCZdg.
National Alliance on Mental Illness. "Mental Health by the Numbers." Retrieved March 2017. http://www.nami.org/Learn-More/Mental-Health-By-the-Numbers.
O*NET OnLine. US Department of Labor. https://www.onetonline.org.
State of Utah, Department of Commerce. "Clinical Mental Health Counselor." Division of Occupational and Professional Licensing application form. Retrieved March 2017. http://www.dopl.utah.gov/apps/CMHC.pdf.
University of Southern California (USC) Suzanne Dworak-Peck School of Social Work "Mental Health Concentration at USC School of Social Work." YouTube, March 4, 2014. http://www.youtube.com/watch?v=oehaP7GDL9M.
US Department of Education. "35th Annual Report to Congress on Implementation of the Individuals with Disabilities Education Act, 2013." May 2014. https://www2.ed.gov/about/reports/annual/osep/2013/parts-b-c/35th-idea-arc.pdf.
US Department of Labor, Bureau of Labor Statistics. *Occupational Outlook Handbook*. https://www.bls.gov/ooh.
Wentworth-Douglass Hospital. "Careers/Behavioral Health Counselor." Job posting, March 7, 2017. https://re22.ultipro.com/WEN1002/JobBoard/JobDetails.aspx?__ID=*5F4E3522239D700B&__jbsrc=F037EEAF-7C64-41B3-AAC2-8125A6D1A8DE.
Yale School of Medicine, Psychiatry. "Yale Psychiatry Residency Program." Retrieved March 2017. http://psychiatry.yale.edu/education/residency.

index

T

U

About the Author

Daniel E. Harmon is the author of numerous books for readers of all ages as well as thousands of magazine and newspaper articles on many subjects. His health-related works include books on Alzheimer's disease, schizophrenia, anorexia nervosa, bipolar disorder, juvenile obesity, overscheduling and stress, and hallucinogens. He lives in Spartanburg, South Carolina.

Photo Credits

Cover, p. 1 (figure) © iStockphoto.com/licsiren; cover, p. 1 (background) Saul Robbins/Corbis/Getty Images; p. 4 Tetra Images/Getty Images; pp. 8–9 Thierry Dosogne/The Image Bank/Getty Images; pp. 10–11 Ocskay Mark/Shutterstock.com; p. 13 Ann Johansson/Corbis Historical/Getty Images; p. 17 The Washington Post/Getty Images; pp. 21, 34–35, 37, 43, 50–51 © AP Images; p. 22 YakobchukOlena/iStock /Thinkstock; pp. 24–25 BSIP/Universal Images Group /Getty Images; pp. 26–27 © iStockphoto.com/asiseeit; pp. 30–31 wavebreakmedia/Shutterstock.com; pp. 39, 40–41 KataryznaBialasiewicz/iStock/Thinkstock; p. 44 Ghislain & Marie David de Lossy/Alamy Stock Photo; p. 46 © asiseeit /E+/Getty Images; p. 53 Alex Raths/iStock/Thinkstock; p. 54 Alexander Raths/Shutterstock.com; pp. 56–57 Ariel Skelley /Blend Images/Getty Images; p. 60 Roman Samborskyi /Shutterstock.com; p. 62 Hero Images/Getty Images; p. 64 David Sacks/Stone/Getty Images.

Design: Matt Cauli; Layout: Tahara Anderson; Senior Editor: Kathy Kuhtz Campbell; Photo Research: Karen Huang